KAY THOMPSON'S ELOISE

Eloise Skates!

STORY BY Lisa McClatchy

ILLUSTRATED BY Tammie Lyon

Ready-to-Read

Aladdin

NEW YORK · LONDON · TORONTO · SYDNEY

ALADDIN PAPERBACKS
An imprint of Simon & Schuster Children's Publishing Division
1230 Avenue of the Americas, New York, NY 10020
Copyright © 2008 by the Estate of Kay Thompson
All rights reserved, including the right of reproduction in whole or in part in any form.
"Eloise" and related marks are trademarks of the Estate of Kay Thompson.
READY-TO-READ, ALADDIN PAPERBACKS, and related logo are
registered trademarks of Simon & Schuster, Inc.
The text of this book was set in Century Old Style.
Manufactured in the United States of America
First Aladdin Paperbacks edition October 2008
8 10 9 7
Library of Congress Control Number: 2007940688
ISBN-13: 978-1-4169-6406-3
ISBN-10: 1-4169-6406-1
0111 LAK

I am Eloise.
I am six.

It is winter.
It is cold.

It is boring.
"Eloise!"
Nanny calls.

"I have a surprise for you!"
"Today we have a date
at the rink."

Maybe winter is
not so boring!

Oh, I love, love,
love to ice-skate!
Weenie and I put on our
winter best.

We'll need warm hats.
And warm coats.

And warm gloves.
And leg warmers, too.

We head down Fifth Avenue.
The stores are all lit up.
There are decorations
everywhere.

The ice rink is all lit up too.

There are lights
on the trees.

And on the flags
along the rink.

"Look, Weenie!" I say.
"It is beautiful!"

Nanny, Weenie, and I
put on our skates.
Nanny wears white.
Weenie wears blue.

My skates match my bow,
of course.
Then we are off!

"Eloise, look out!" Nanny
cries as I narrowly miss
the pretty lady.

"Eloise, watch out!" Nanny cries as I narrowly duck between the couple holding hands.

"Eloise, watch out!" Nanny cries as I weave through the crowd of tourists.

"It is okay, Nanny!" I cry.

Watch me twirl for the tourists!

Watch me glide by the tree!

Watch me jump into
the air. . . .

"Oops!" says Nanny.
"Oops!" says the policeman.

"Oops!" I say.
"Thanks for catching me,"
  I say.

"Eloise, I think we need
hot chocolate," Nanny says.

Oh, I love, love,
love to skate!